The Old Man

by
Robert J Brennan

Copyright © 2025 Robert J Brennan

ISBN: 978-1-917778-18-3

All rights reserved, including the right to reproduce this book, or portions thereof in any form. No part of this text may be reproduced, transmitted, downloaded, decompiled, reverse engineered, or stored, in any form or introduced into any information storage and retrieval system, in any form or by any means, whether electronic or mechanical without the express written permission of the author.

For my all of my grandchildren and to Lesley my sweet precious wife.

Introduction
The Old man's forest now more of a wood than a forest as swathes of the tall Scots-pines that gave the forest its canopy was lost during the great storm of 1987. The remaining trees including the majestic great oak that stands within the forest clearing a haven for the many animals and birds that call the old forest their home. The future of the forest now in doubt as all around farms are being sold as housing development creeps across the meadows, but for today the wildlife go about their daily business.

Bertie the badger
Bertie a familiar face around the forest and always out scrounging food to the annoyance of the other inhabitants left his home in a nearby county several years back and laments about having to give it up. It was lovely nothing to be heard but the sound of cattle grazing in the field and food was a plenty with the dung everywhere. Then one-night Im laying on my bed reading me newspaper when suddenly the whole place is a blaze with lights and snarling dogs and I had to leave in a jiffy. Made my way to this here place and settled down in the far corner away from all those garlic things that pop up each spring. Think old Dr Brown the owl said they were called ransoms or something, yuk. I would pay a ransom to be away from them. I keep my distance from that place when they pop up and yet them lot never seem bothered by the smell as he nods towards the rookery.

The rookery
The rookery on the outskirts of the forest has been there for as long as the other inhabitants can remember and quite chaotic in early spring with a mad flurry of noise and nest building. Ruby one of the most senior of the rooks spends her days hopping from tree to tree reminding the young Branchers of the bad old days when they could end up in a rook and rabbit pie if straying too close to the farm and found stealing grain. Not all the juveniles heed the warning and fly off to the farm fields where they sit brazenly on the

outstretched arms of the scarecrow before swooping down on the grain. Several of their number are shot and left dangling from a nearby fence as a warning to other would be thieves. Well says Bertram from his vantage point in the tallest tree in the rookery, it is clear they no longer eat rook pie. But not rabbit pie says Ruby, tipping her wing to indicate a poacher with a brace of rabbits over his shoulder.

They should take a leaf out of Maple the rabbits book says Bertram, she doesn't let her kits wander and they only play in the meadow at the forest edge.

He has several greys as well hanging from his belt says Ruby.

Bertram recalled his younger days when red squirrels were a plenty in the forest before the march of the greys, now only a small colony of reds remained over by the rabbit warren. I must say says Bertram, I really do not have much time for those greys, nothing but rodents with bushy tails. How on earth can people delight in eating them?

Still says Ruby, it is very sad even though the greys can be troublesome for us too.

The discarded apple cores

Apple cores who dropped the apple cores asks Maple bunny, mother of Alfalfa, Angelica and Ash, who on earth would drop apple cores?

Good mornings Miss Maple said Bertie the badger

Did you do this Mr Bertie? me um no says Bertie, picking up one of the cores before popping it into his mouth and swallowing 'a tasty morsel but where did it come from? asks Bertie.

I know' says Spudgy the sparrow 'I seen two geezers and their massive dog walkin along the edgerow and they tossed over the cores'

Edgerow asks Maple' 'he means hedgerow says Bertie, it's his cockney accent, can hardly understand a word out of his beak'.

Anyways; says Smudgy, 'can't be hanging round here all day me old china plate Im off to the farm house for a butcher's see if any seeds been put out'

Off Smudgy flew across the meadow whistling 'maybe it's because Im a Londoner.

China plate, butchers what on earth was he going on about? asks Maple

Well says Bertie, I was collecting worms from a pile of compost at the farm and got talking to old red the rooster when Spudgy turned up chirping on about something that had me totally lost. When Spudgy got off, old red gave me the rundown it's called cockney rhyming slang, china plate is mate, butchers I think is butchers hook meaning look.

Well I will never understand him nor do I seek to understand, why on earth couldn't he just say simply mate or friend and look, instead of all that rhyming says a puzzled Maple

Cockney rhyming says Bertie

Quite says Maple gazing up at the gathering clouds looks like rain again Mr Bertie I will have to be getting home to get my sheets in and get the carrot stew on the stove before the kits arrive home from school.

Darn rain says Bertie me don't like getting wet but at least it brings the worms out, so there's me dinner sorted

Urgh says Maple 'I shall be on my way'

'By zee bye then' says Bertie

New neighbours

Gather around all says Doctor Brown the wise old owl as he sat perched outside his home in the majestic oak tree. 'We have a new family moved into the forest and they are here to make everyone acquaintance

Come, come forward don't be shy' says Dr Brown as he ushered the new family into the circle of animals and birds.

Hi Im Jack the Stoat and this is my wife Jill'

Hi Im also called Jack, but Jack by the hedge' says shrew

Why Jack by the hedge? asks Jill

I don't really know, ever since I can remember I have been known as Jack by the hedge, I think it might be because Im always scurrying in and out of the hedgerow'

I think there is a plant called Jack by the hedge; says Jill

I do believe that maybe true says Dr Brown I will just look in my big book of 'all things' Jack, Jack, aah here it is Jack by the hedge Alliaria petiolata or garlic mustard

Yuk says Bertie I hate garlic, don't know how that old red rooster can cover his snails in it

It's a French delicacy says Jack the stoat and used all the time in the restaurant we lived above in New Orleans.

New Orleans' gasped Maple what on earth where you doing in New Orleans and how did you get here?

Oh, said Jack rather easy to explain we belonged to a couple of town people, nice they were and really looked after us. We would catch rats for them and one day while out ratting a massive big tabby cat, huge it was appeared from nowhere and we had to flee for our lives

It was horrible' says Jill

Horrible it most certainly was' said Jack and it didn't stop chasing us till we ran up a plank onto a ship where we thought to lay low for a few hours. Tired as we were through all the running and dodging the huge beast we fell asleep and when we woke up all we could see was water in every direction

Tired interrupted Bertie, I thought you stoats were all fit

Ignore him, pray do continue says Dr Brown

Well said Jack we were all at sea and after weeks of hiding on the boat and sneaking around for scraps of food we finally arrived at some port and got off the boat and hitched a ride in the back of a truck full of eggs and ended up somewhere in that direction pointing back across the meadow in the direction of the farm house.

Fascinating' says Ecclefechan the hare who had joined the circle sporting his tartan cravat

fascinating indeed, did I ever tell you all about my great, great, great uncle Bonnie Prince hare escaping in a boat

Yes, came the gatherings response

Well did I tell you about, Yes, you have responded the gathering

Dr Brown fluttering his feathers in annoyance adds we have heard those tales more times than we care to recall, turning to Jack and Jill, welcome to the community my learned and much travelled friends

Excuse me says Jack by the hedge, but don't stoats eat shrews?

And rabbits gulped Maple

Erm well yes that is an unfortunate part of a stoat's diet but you are quite safe around us because we are pescatarian says Jack

Pesca what? asks Maple

Pescatarian said Jill we only eat fish

You mean you don't eat meat asks Jack by the hedge but you said you were catching rats

We were, we catch em but we don't eat em' says Jack we just hand them over and get paid for every rats tail, what happens to them after that we don't know

This is all very strange, very strange indeed, stoats that only eat fish says Dr Brown, well there is plenty of fish in the river so you won't go hungry

And so, the animals in turn shook the hands of Jack and Jill and went about their daily business. Bruce the hedgehog was the last to be introduced to the newcomers. Hi Im Quillis though my friends call me Bruce, I don't care too much for the day times too much traffic and noise but I heard newcomers had arrived so I set my alarm clock to be here and thought as Im having to be up mighty early I may as well take the opportunity to get me some grubs and worms.

The early bird catches the worm said Jill, what? says Bruce there was no birds out at that time.

No what I meant says Jill, oh never mind.

I managed to get quite a bag full says Bruce but I never expected the brock to be out there that early, no I never.

Lurking under an elderberry bush he was and when my back was turned he grabbed my bag and even had the cheek to say thanks Brucie. No one calls me Brucie and laughing ever so loudly so he was as he ran away, shouting Brucie bonus whatever that meant.

Well I never, said Jill, very sorry to hear that says Jack but it was nice to meet with you under the circumstances.

Sylvester the fox

Ecclefechan the hare was just about to leave the woods to cross the meadow to the carrot fields when he spotted Sylvester the fox.

Morning Sly me old mate

'It's Mr Sylvester to you barked the fox

Whatever replied Ecclefechan anyways you missed all the news, we've got new kids on the block, as they say'

As who says? asks Sylvester

As they say replies Ecclefechan

Yes, you said that but who exactly my dim-witted oversized rabbit are they?

Erm don't rightly know but the new family, they are from New Orleans

How exciting replies Sylvester as he yawns and walks on, stopping momentarily to gaze at a parliament of magpies cawing at each other in a distant Sycamore tree. That time of the year already muses Sylvester, sorting out the hierarchy of the tribe no doubt.

Morning Mrs magpie, how's your family' says Ecclefechan

I've heard it all now says Sylvester shaking his head, greeting magpies what has this world come too and how on earth do you know which one of those is the mother?

You say it when you see more than one, if not its bad luck' say Ecclefechan

It will be bad luck for them if I get my paws on them, the despicable creatures, anyway be off with you I can't be seen standing around here all morning talking to an oversize rabbit I have my reputation to think off.

Im a hare not a rabbit says Ecclefechan shaking his head anyway I shall go and speak to our new family they are right brainy pair of stoats'

Stoats! barks Sylvester

Why didn't you say they were stoats' then a sudden realization crosses his mind and closing his eyes he forlornly thinks.

If it weren't for that stupid rule the daft old owl introduced about living in peace and harmony and keeping the decorum of the wood I could be enjoying a stoat sandwich for lunch.

They are pescatarian' says Ecclefechan

Yes, I know they are pesky' remarks Sylvester annoyingly

Not pesky, pescatarian, meaning that they only eat fish,

What! Said Sylvester stoats that only east fish, the worlds gone mad. Don't know about the world thing said Ecclefechan but Dr Brown was okay with it and told them there's plenty of fish in the river'

Did he now' says Sylvester, well maybe he ought to be having that conversation with old Harry the heron, I mean here Iam relaxing in the meadow trying to catch some sunrays when the big clumsy thing drops down beside me, blabbing on and on about how the eels are getting more slippery and having not seen a trout in weeks'

Come to think of it' says Ecclefechan I seen him the other day he didn't look himself at all stood in the river on one leg and when I came past a few hours later he was still glumly standing in the same spot.

I waved to him but he just took off without a word not even a goodbye, damn blooming rude if you ask me.

Maybe' yawns Sylvester he did not have time to hear you tell one of your highland tales and how your ancestor Rupert hare of Dumbarton defeated the English crown

Remind me my rabbit like friend how did Rupert defeat the English crown, Im intrigued to learn

Well says Ecclefechan it was a dark moonless night, nothing stirred in the woods no sound could be heard not even an owl as all around slept

I suspect not all says Sylvester, dear Rupert was no doubt awake

How did you know that asks Ecclefechan in amazement?

Process of elimination my dear rabbit, process of elimination

Ecclefechan picked up a thin fallen branch and pretended to be in a sword fight with an imaginary foe, yield I say yield.

The imaginary sword fight ending abruptly with a loud rumbling noise heading towards them through the undergrowth and coming to a screeching stop.

Hamilton the wild boar

What on earth is going on? barks Sylvester wiping soil from his clothes, you can pay the cleaning bill

Im being chased says Hamilton panting loudly, Im sweating like a pig

You are a pig remarks Sylvester and a fat lazy one at that, who on earth would be chasing you?

The people from the town they want me for a hog roast, I was rolling around in a patch of mud when I heard voices in the distance. I ignored it at first then they got louder and louder and closer and closer till there they were with big coloured sticks in their hands making towards me so I run as fast as my legs could carry me, look at me I'm trembling, trembling I don't think I will ever recover.

Hmm this I have to see' says Sylvester, they are usually on horses and have those pesky dogs running around in front of them. So, off the three of them went following the route that Hamilton had taken. After walking for about half an hour, Hamilton shouts there they are, and so, they were towns people, lots of them walking hither and thither. They were as Hamilton said all carrying coloured sticks that they placed in the ground in different places, pulling them out and repeating the process whilst looking through a strange object on three sticks.

What do you think they are doing with those sticks, says Ecclefechan, seems they cannot decide where to leave them?

They could be searching for warrens and dens says Sylvester.

Maybe they don't know where to put their barbecue says Hamilton

Well they are from the town remarked Sylvester but what do they want in that field and why so many, there is only one thing for it we will have to go and see that daft old owl' as much as it pains me to ask him, he will likely know.

As they turned to walk back the way they came Ecclefechan said 'I spy with my little eye something beginning with T'

Tree yawned Sylvester

Ah got you there says Ecclefechan, what tree, there's plenty of trees so what tree did I spy?

Pointing towards the forest, Sylvester says that one

Damn how did you know it was that one, okay then I spy with my little eye

Wait a moment says Sylvester I've just won, it's my turn now you thick rabbit like thing, hmm let me see aah I spy with my little eye something beginning with B

Something beginning with B, no you have me there said Ecclefechan scratching his head.

Buzzard says Sylvester pointing up to the sky as a buzzard hovered over them.

Yikes screamed Ecclefechan who took off to the safety of the forest.

That got rid of him remarked Sylvester, turning to Hamilton now my lardy friend how about you sniffing me out some truffles.

Wille the weasel

Meanwhile Jack and Jill were busy furnishing their new home with reed mats when there was a rap, rap, rap on the door.

Who can that be asks Jill, we are not expecting visitors. Jack opened the door and is met by Willie the weasel, holding a few pansy flowers that he hands over to Jill.

G'day cousins, how ya going? Im Willie.

What says Jack, we are not going anywhere we have only just arrived

Strewth, say Willie, I came along here to welcome you both, I was a newcomer once and not so long back my home is down under.

What says Jack under our feet?

Ignoring the question Willie sits himself down in a corner of the house and says two sugars for me and easy on the chocolate fudge cake Im watching my weight.

Jack asks again, is your home under our feet?

Not under your feet says Willie, down under, you know Oz, Australia you must have heard of it, boomerangs and all that.

I came over here with a load of sheep felt like a change but rain, rain, blooming rain all the time. I've had my fair share of this place and looking to make my way back home if I can just find a way to get there.

You might need to travel to a town by the sea and sneak on board a boat says Jill

Nah too risky walking around a town too many feral cats and dogs say Willie

They must have cats and dogs where you came from says Jack

Australia, Oz says Willie it's mainly horses and sheep but there are wild dogs, Dingo's they call em and they snoop around but the people at the farm scare them off, vicious beggars they are.

Who the people say Jill?

No not the people they are friendly enough if you don't bother them, it's the Dingo's, hunt in packs they do, vicious beggars.

You got to be careful as well with shipping says Willie, I had a cobber once, polecat Pete and he got on board one of the ships, problem was Pete was always a bit of a drongo and got on an ice breaker ship to Antarctica never heard from him since.

Cobber, drongo remarks Jill

Yep cobber, mate and drongo you know idiot

How do you know he got on that ship? asks Jack

Chas the crow told me, said he seen him boarding the ship and just before it sailed Chas was mooching around looking for tucker and noticed all the boxes had Antarctica on em.

Whose Tucker asks Jill, was he lost?

Tuckers not a person its grub says Willie and that dear cousins were hooroo to Pete, anyway what you two doing here, so far from home.

Jack starts to recite the story of how they came to the forest when Jill says excuse me for a minute Isn't Antarctica the South pole?

Sure, is says Willie, place is just full of penguins and seals no place for a polecat. That's it, can't you see says Jill, Pete the polecat has gone back to his home in the pole

Strewth says Willie never thought of that, just goes to show you learn something new every day.

Dr Brown

Doctor Brown has lived in the forest for longer than he can remember with the majestic oak tree being home to generations of Tawny owls. The forest and surrounding fields and meadow home also to Smalls the little owl and McConaughoot the barn owl or Matt as he likes to be addressed. None of them however are as educated as Dr Brown who is the fountain of all wisdom and knowledge.

Dr Brown no longer swoops across the fields and the meadow and prefers to stay around his home in the majestic oak were he often entertains visitors from the owl community. However, he despairs of the conversations he holds with Matt who to the annoyance of Dr Brown uses the word owl in every sentence.

Owl of a sudden Dr Brown I was sat perched there nothing to eat for days when a whole hoard of rats came scurrying from the barn as the hay was being moved, my freezer was full for weeks owl things come to those who wait.

Quite says Dr Brown and for owl intent and purposes, drat you have me using that word now. He was just about to discuss the vocabulary with Matt when he is distracted by movement in the clearance. What brings this motley bunch here he says, as Sylvester, Hamilton and Ecclefechan come into view?

Good afternoon your most esteem lord and majesty, your graciousness says Sylvester we come bearing gifts or rather news from afar, well from the fields by the meadow to be precise.

Get on with it Sylvester you know Im too busy for your poor attempt at wit.

They're going to be having barbecues on the meadow shouts Hamilton

Barbecues on the meadow? asks Dr Brown

Take no notice of the pig says Sylvester but something strange is certainly a foot informing Dr Brown of what they had all witnessed.

I was nearly a buzzard's supper said Ecclefechan, it kept swooping and diving, swooping and diving trying to seize me in its talons. I could hear the beating of its wings and I felt its breath on the fur on my neck.

I had to zig zag all across the meadow, I tell you it took all my innermost strength and guile to escape it.

Alas says Sylvester it was already thinking of what sauce to baste you in and salivating at the prospect of 'Hare a la royale'

Ecclefechan gulped and tried to speak but no sound came from his mouth.

He wasn't chased! shouts Hamilton looking across to Sylvester, we both seen the buzzard just fly off so what's he going on about?

The pig proclaims the truth says Sylvester, what we have here is a feeble attempt to put a modern spin on the classic Rupert hare of Dumbarton myth.

Why do you call me a pig Im a wild boar not a pig? asks Hamilton

I concede that you are a boar says Sylvester, a very boring boar, however the only difference my fat friend between you and the late Porky Bess from the farm is your meat is said to be more intense and far richer.

Bess was a delightful sow says Hamilton, I remember her well

I heard she was partial to apple sauce said Sylvester

Dr Brown! shouts Hamilton, I must protest he is trying to cause me alarm and undue distress.

Stop this nonsense now Sylvester and Im not for one minute interested in the alleged heroics of the hare Says Dr Brown. Now tell me again these objects they were looking through had three sticks under them?

Yep says Sylvester

I will just look in my book of 'all things' says Dr Brown.
Aah yes found it, the people of the town call it a theodolite which is a measuring instrument for surveying.
Now what could they be possibly surveying, hmmm I will need more information before I can give an informed opinion on this matter.

That's that then, the owl doesn't know says Ecclefechan

Well he wants more information, says Hamilton but Im not going anywhere near those fields in case they are surveying the best place to hold a barbecue with me the guest of honour.

'Roti De porc De Dijon' remarks Sylvester

Dr Brown, he is at it again, shouts Hamilton

Marquis Morningcall

Red the rooster was sat in his usual spot on the fence overlooking the hen house with one eyed closed, trying to catch a few winks when he was disturbed by the familiar but annoying Spudgy

Hello red me ole mate how's it going, what's with all the box of toys? pointing with his right wing to the fields at the far side of the farm

Red who had long given up on Spudgy addressing him by his title Marquis Morningcall opened his shut eye, shook his feathers and addressed Spudgy.

Good afternoon Mon spudge.

Err its Spudgy not spudge remarked the sparrow

Yes, indeed Mon Spudgy, you are enquiring of the noise yes?

Yep what's with the box of toys then says Spudgy.

Thee boxes of toys as you say is thee people of the town who are going to build new homes across thee meadow and neighbouring fields.

I fear Mon Spudgy that thee farm house might also be going so Im a little occupied with finding new homes for the chickens and hens.

Blimey says Spudgy does that mean the townies will have homes all over the place.

Yes, indeed Mon Spudgy it is my belief, that the farmer is selling up, it is as you say a matter of bees and honey.

Red was familiar with Spudgy rhyming slang and was able to converse with Spudgy.

Always about money says Spudgy, ere does old Brown know what's going on?

I have not engaged in conversation with Monsieur Dr Brown for some time so you may want to deliver my message to him.

What message is that asks Smudgy?

My message Mon spudge

Err Spudgy

Yes of course Mon Spudgy, my message is simple, thee occupants of thee wood will need to be on the move and sourcing new abodes.

Abodes asks Smudgy puzzled?

Yes, Mon Spudgy abodes, you know Micky Mouse's

You mean houses why didn't you just say so remarks Spudgy

And off Spudgy flew to bring the news to Dr Brown who had just retired to his hole in the tree to have his afternoon nap.

News of the development to come

Oy Brownie shouts Spudgy I ave a message from red the rooster

Oh no what now says Dr Brown I have only just got rid of those other fools

Hi Spudgy shouts Leonard the Linnet

Hi Lenny me old mate how's the family?

Doing okay Spudgy, new uns due in a few days waiting for the eggs to hatch.

What do you want says Dr Brown fastening his dressing gown it better be good for your sake?

Old red the rooster said to bring you his message

Don't you mean the Marquis Morningcall said Dr Brown

Yes, him says Spudgy, he said the towns people are going to build Mickey Mouse's all over the meadow and you lot in the forest have to have it away on your toes.

Micky Mouse's, have it away on our toes, what are you going on about, what is this message from the Marquis Morningcall?

That's it says Spudgy Mickey Mouse's or abodes he said and you lot having to be on the move and source new ones

New ones of what says Dr Brown

New abodes replied Spudgy

Im lost Mr Spudgy, I haven't a clue what you are talking about I will have to call on the Marquis Morningcall myself once I have dressed.

Dr Brown hurriedly dressed and flew to the farm

Good afternoon Marquis Morningcall how are you on this fine warm afternoon.

Im very well Monsieur Dr Brown but surprised to see you here sounding so chirpy under thee circumstances.

Well says Dr Brown I was just turning in for my afternoon nap when that annoying sparrow came shouting outside my front door and rambling on about some fictitious mouse and his abode.

I fear Monsieur Dr Brown that thee news was not imparted very well to you but alas it is not good news at all.

Settling down on the fence post Dr Brown listened intently as the Marquis Morningcall delivered the alarming news.

Well this simply won't do says Dr Brown it won't do at all and I will not stand for this. The forest has stood for centuries and is not just my ancestral home but the ancestral home of all the animals and birds in that forest.

Well apart from a couple of stoats, a weasel the badger and those annoying grey squirrels.

Still an all it is their adopted home, and off Dr Brown flew to deliver the news to the inhabitants of the forest.

Maurice the moorhen

Maurice was lazing about on the pond when all of a sudden, a large plume of water shot up into the air the ripple sending him sailing across the pond.

Good grief what on earth was that.

Seconds later Harry the heron appears from under the water

Excuse me, excuse me this is no place for a heron

What says Harry I don't see a sign that says no fishing allowed?

Well, well there isn't a sign as such but this here pond is only for medium size water birds not oversized waders like you.

Needs must say's Harry, no fish in the river

No fish in the river says Maurice that's highly unlikely the river is teaming with fish so it is.

Well said Harry the river is dry and Im now having to source my lunch from these farm land ponds and Im not accustomed to eating carp the scales get stuck in my beak.

Im not at all happy with this says Maurice Im going to have to speak to Dr Brown to investigate this, this outrage, this invasion.

At which Harry flies off without a word or goodbye.

Maurice sits in the reeds to momentarily compose himself then makes his way to see Dr Brown.

Dr Brown meanwhile is engaged in conversation with Matt the barn owl

And so, says Matt if the farm goes so does my home in the barn so we are owl in this together.

Dr Brown, Dr Brown may I have a word it is rather urgent and quite upsetting

Yes of course Maurice, do excuse me Matt, owl be in touch, drat there it goes again.

Well Maurice it is good o see you but you do not normally stray away from your pond, in the farm land.

It's that heron Harry he came diving into my pond like a meteorite had landed said he has to resort to fishing his suppers in the farm ponds now because the river is empty of fish.

The river is not empty of fish, says Dr Brown in fact only the other day I was telling our new family the stoats from New Orleans that they will never go hungry because of the abundance of fish in the river. They said they were going to dine out by the river with it being a lovely evening and they have not been back to complain of there being no fish.

In fact, Matt remarked on the smell of smoked trout coming from the stoat's home so they must have caught quite a few.

What! said Maurice why are stoats eating fish?

They are Pescatarian and only eat fish, how remarkable, stoats that only eat fish said Dr Brown. Now regarding Harry and the fishing rights I will get word to him to cease and desist his behaviour but I do have more pressing matters to be getting on with so I must fly.

Thanks Dr Brown says Maurice I shall leave it with you.

As Maurice was flying low across the farm land back to the pond he heard a shout from below, looking down it was Arthur the Mallard.

Hi Maurice you won't believe what happened before, we were just out with the ducklings teaching them to swim when whoosh a big fountain of water.

Don't tell me say Maurice, Harry the heron

Yes, says Arthur, we told him in no uncertain terms what we thought of his frightening the ducklings and all that.

Well says Maurice I have submitted a formal complaint to Dr Brown.

Look says Arthur there he is now swooping in on another pond

Right says Maurice he is for it now, are you with me Arthur

Sure, am Maurice, and off they went to confront the heron who was stood with one leg in the pond.

Oh, hello says Harry

Don't give us hello say Maurice, I have complained to Dr Brown about your conduct unbecoming.

And you frightened the ducklings says Arthur, they will be having nightmares for years to come.

It's not nice feeling hungry says Harry and if the river is empty I have no choice than to visit the ponds and I don't really care for the fish in the ponds but needs must.

Well says Maurice, Dr Brown said the new stoat family had no problem getting fish from the river

Stoats getting fish says Harry what for?

Apparently says Maurice they only eat fish, yes, I know quite strange but that is how it is.

Well says Harry I don't understand it at all I have been trying catch eels and trout to no avail for weeks.

Well says Arthur why don't we go to the river and see whether we can see any fish and try and sort this unnecessary business out without the need for further litigation.

Litigation? asks Harry, yes says Arthur legal action to stop you doing what you have been doing.

Right says Maurice lets go to the river and off they all flew.

Look says Maurice there's tons of fish, and eels says Arthur, where? asks Harry I can't see a thing.

Look says Maurice there's a trout right by your feet, and another and another.

Where? asks Harry, I can't see anything its all just murky water.

Harry, says Arthur can you read that sign on the river bank?

Well yes of course, it says N, or is it M, no its an N then Q or is it an O.

Harry that's the problem says Maurice, when did you last have your eyes tested?

Well says Harry I think it was a few summers back

Well said Arthur you need to go and make an appointment with Oscar the ophthalmic otter for an eye test.

I will do that first thing in the morning said Harry

The magical spectacles

Late the following afternoon Sylvester was relaxing in the meadow when there was a loud flapping of wings as Harry settled down beside him.

Not again says Sylvester without opening his eyes, what is it this time the frogs have stopped hopping and the newts are nowhere to be seen?

Newts? said Harry I have never seen those fellows around these parts?

Apparently, said Sylvester, there is a whole colony of them over that way somewhere pointing to the far side of the forest.

I have never wanted to try one even as an appetizer said Harry, it has been passed down through generations of the heron family right back to my great, great uncle Bartholomew of Norfolk that we give them a wide berth.

Exciting yarns Sylvester

I can see wood ants carrying leaves said Harry and look a dung beetle and how vibrant is the shell of the ladybirds. Do you know Sylvester I have never really appreciated how beautiful things around us are including the trout with its colours that look like a rainbow?

Maybe yarns Sylvester that is why they are called rainbow trout, anyway what on earth are you blabbing on about, can't a fox get some peace and quiet.

Opening his eyes, he turns annoyingly to look at Harry, good grief says Sylvester shaking his head, Im seeing things. Rubbing both of his eyes he looks again at Harry, no I did not imagine it the heron is wearing spectacles.

What on earth are you doing with them on he asks? Do you like them replied Harry? I got them from the opticians it seems I was wrong about the fish and eels I just couldn't see them properly. These spectacles are magical I can see everything even that ant on your cravat.

Urgh says Sylvester swatting the ant from his cravat, get off me

I would encourage everyone to get a pair says Harry they give you the vision of a hawk.

Do they now said Sylvester, I think that my dear friend Ecclefechan would be keen to hear that, he has quite an interest in hawks?

I shall immediately go and tell him says Harry

Yes, he will be delighted says Sylvester do give him my regards, adding that reminds me Oscar still has my pie dish.

Reginald the rabbit
Reginald was making his way home to the warren which stretches out below the fallen scots pines now covered in fungi and ferns.

Oh, how I love this time of year thinks Reginald

Evening Reggie shouts Peck- a- lot the woodpecker

Evening Peckers nice evening for it

Peck-a-lot winked and carried on drilling a hole in the tree

What the blazes is that racket asks Harlow the red squirrel? It's that woodpecker again replies Paramour he is on that scots pine by the rabbit warren.

Such anti-social behaviour says Harlow why doesn't he go and do it somewhere else, preferably where those greys hang out.

I think he is finished for the day said Paramour he has flown off.

Peace at last said Harlow, pass me a hazelnut please Paramour.

Reginald turned the corner to the warren where Maple and the kits are waiting to welcome him home.

Welcome home Reg says Maple I was just about to put the kits to bed but seen you coming around the corner.

Reginald kissed the three kits and told them he shall be up to tell them a bedtime story in a few minutes.

Can we have the one about the tree bears said Ash

Of course, says Reginald, I shall be up shortly.

I was thinking of taking a few days off work so we can visit my sister and her family says Reginald.

Oh yes that will be lovely says Maple the kits will enjoy meeting their cousins again, by the way there is a lovely new couple in the forest, Jack and Jill Stoat.

Stoat! Says Reginald in the forest?

Yes, says Maple but they are not like the stoats that we were warned about when we were kits, these only eat fish.

Really? asks Reginald, I find that hard to believe.

They are pescatarians says Maple

Pesca what? Says Reginald, Pescatarian replies Maple, look it's here in the dictionary

Well I never said Reginald who would ever have guessed that, certainly one for the quiz night.

I better go and tell the bedtime story otherwise they won't sleep.

The following morning with it not being a school day the kits are picking wild flowers in the meadow at the forest edge.

Don't pick too many Bluebells say Maple they are there for everyone to enjoy and Dr Brown will get very cross if you pick a lot. And do not pick any of those flowers that look like bees no matter how nice they will look in a jar they are only there for a short time, that is why all the animals and the birds visit when they are in flower.

They do look like bees says Angelica. That is how they got their name says Maple, Dr Brown said they are called Bee orchids and those over there are called ghost orchids.

Dr Brown said they only flower every 10 years so we are fortunate to see them in bloom.

Maple, shouts Reginald we are all asked to be at the old oak midday as Dr Brown has some important news to tell us. I wonder what it is says Maple, perhaps another family have come to the forest, but then when Jack and Jill came the other day Dr Brown sent a note for us to meet the new family. Well there is no mention of a new family at all in this note says Reginald, it must be really important because he says it is a matter of the highest importance and every effort should be made to attend.

The meeting

All the animals and birds had gathered and await Dr Brown

Wonder what it's all about asks Bertie

Maybe it's about you stealing things that dont belong to you says Bruce and what was all that Brucie bonus thing about?

Bertie, ignoring Bruce turned to Harry I like the specs Harry they make you look quite important.

Dignified says Bertram the rook

Just then the tree house door opens and out came Dr Brown accompanied by Matt the barn owl and the red rooster Marquis Morningcall

Welcome to you all says Dr Brown

bon après - midi says Marquis Morningcall

He means good afternoon says Spudgy who had joined the gathering crowd

We only have one item to discuss says Matt and that is why you have owl been asked here today, I shall now hand you back to Dr Brown.

Thank you, Matt, thank you the Marquis Morningcall

Wot about me? says Spudgy for the translation like, and why is there no Rosie Lee?

We do not have time to drink thee tea says the Marquis Morningcall

Right back to the business of the day says Dr Brown it is my solemn and sad duty to inform you that this forest and the meadow is at risk of being torn down with no tree left standing and no ponds in the fields.

What! says Hamilton where will I hide

It is not just a case of where you will hide says Dr Brown it is where will we go if we are to be chased from this our home.

Can we not challenge it says Reginald?

No Im afraid not says Dr Brown we are as they say up the creek without a paddle.

As who says? asks Sylvester, adding these whoever they are have a lot to say none of which makes an ounce of sense to me.

It is what it is, says the Marquis Morningcall

What is it asks Bertie?

It is a saying Mon Bertie, Cest comme ca

Barney Rubble says Spudgy

Who on earth is Barney Rubble? asks Sylvester

He means thee trouble says the Marquis Morningcall

Never mind all this Barney Rubble says Matt we need to form a plan of action we need to be organised or we will end up owl over the place.

Thank you, Matt says Dr Brown owl take over now, drat that word again.

You must be vigilante my dear friends and let us know if you see any towns people in the meadow or coming into the forest and they will be carrying coloured sticks and things that they will look through.

We shall take turns to watch, Ecclefechan as you can run fast you shall watch from the meadow, Maurice you and Arthur can watch from the ponds and Harry you can watch the river.

Splendid says Harry, my spectacles will allow me to see anyone approaching along the river bank.

I shall watch the far side of the forest says Reginald, the warren will need to be on full alert.

Bertie you can patrol at night says Dr Brown and I shall also fly around the forest at dusk.

As long as I dont have to go near those garlic ransom things says Bertie

This is ever so exciting says Ecclefechan, and reminds me of my ancestor

Not now Ecclefechan says Dr Brown

Sylvester, you have not volunteered your service, says Dr Brown

Well I can be the quartermaster says Sylvester, make sure we have enough supplies and hand out the rations to everyone with the exception of the pig that is, pointing at Hamilton.

Dr Brown, I cannot go without rations I need to eat like everyone else says Hamilton.

But not eat the equivalent of everyone else says Sylvester

Will you two stop this petty squabble that you have going on, says Dr Brown.

Im for drawing a line under it says Hamilton

And yourself? Sylvester asks Dr Brown

How very strange I had a dream last night about a line says Sylvester

A dream? asks Dr Brown

Yes, says Sylvester it is a bit hazy but becoming clearer aah yes, I can see it now it wasn't a line it was a loin, a loin of pork chops Chez Le Reve Francais.

Damn it says Dr Brown, Hamilton just ignore him.

Right then says Dr Brown we all know what we are doing so look lively and let us be getting on with the task ahead.

Does this mean that school will be closed asked Maple?

I think we all need to be remaining close to each other so Im closing the school for the foreseeable future says Dr Brown

I remember my owl school having to close once says Matt

I never knew there was a school just for owls says Dr Brown

It wasn't said Matt all sorts of creatures attended it

But you just said your owl school, drat you meant your old school says Dr Brown

That's what I said replied Matt my owl school

On that note, said Dr Brown, creatures of the forest to your duties

Enemy at the gates

Reginald the rabbit came running into the clearance by the majestic oak banging a wooden spoon on a tin plate, alert, alert, thumping his right paw on the ground, alert

All of the animals and birds came rushing to the clearance

Dr Brown appeared from the majestic oak, what is happening

People Dr Brown walking around the outskirts of the forest and around the meadow with viewing things that they are pointing at the trees said Reginald

They pointed one of the darn things at me said Bertie, there were a couple of them and one shouted look a badger so I took cover in the undergrowth till they had gone.

How did they get this close without being spotted said Dr Brown, where was Ecclefechan, he was supposed to be watching the meadow? Alas says Sylvester the oversize rabbit is snoozing in the meadow I have just passed him and he is already charging the enemy guns in his dreams. This simply won't do says Dr Brown, we could have all been snared as the hare slept.

Dr Brown shouts Maple as she came running into the clearance with her three kits. What has happened said Dr Brown? are you and the kits okay said Reginald? Yes, we are very well, the people that came are not trying to harm us they were smiling and saying how lovely the kits were, and none of them had coloured sticks.

We can vouch for that said Harlow the red squirrel, they gave me and Paramour a whole bag of mixed nuts to share. And they even chased away the greys when they tried to steal the bag said Paramour.

It could be a trick said Bertie, towns people are as sly as a fox

I beg your pardon said Sylvester, cunning, but never sly Im open and transparent in all of my dealings. At least pointing at Bertie, I can wander around as I choose whatever the time of day or night.

I can too, said Bertie

Poppycock said Sylvester, poor old Daisy the Jersey cow gets the jitters every time she gets a mere glimpse of you and takes off to the barn like she has just heard the starter pistol for the 100 metres sprint.

It's all a myth said Bertie, we aint a risk to cows

Stop this now said Dr Brown, this is getting us nowhere, we must find out what the good town people are doing they could be are only hope.

Ecclefechan came into the clearance and announces that it is all quiet in the meadow. Apart from your snoring said Sylvester which masked the sound of the hordes of town people rampaging across the meadow. However, I do concur it is now all quiet on the western front.

What is he going on about? asks Ecclefechan

Well Ecclefechan as you slept, town people were wandering around the outskirts of the forest having crossed the meadow. Fortunately, no harm was done, they appear to be friendly but you are now relieved of your duties.

Over the course of the next few weeks things returned to normal and there was no sign of any hostile activity within the fields so Dr Brown declared the current state of emergency over.

One morning Spudgy flew across to the farm house to give Monsieur Morningcall the Sunday news

Morning red me ole mate says Spudgy

Good morning Mon Spudge

It's Spudgy

Ah yes Mon Spudgy do forgive me, how can I be of service.

I was just enjoying some grub over at the Plough Inn and I could hear all the chatter from the near and far

You mean from the bar Mon Spudgy

Yeah that's what I just said, the near and far, do keep up red. It seems red me ole mate that new towns people are taking over the farm. Old Jonesy and his trouble is upping sticks. Wot was it they were saying, yeah something about re-wilding the place whatever that means.

Im not quite with you Mon Spudgy sometimes it is very hard to follow what you are saying. Perhaps that is the reason why thee farmer Mr Jones is selling up because he is in financial trouble.

I don't know anything about any money problems says Spudgy.

But Mon Spudgy you just said thee farmer is moving with his trouble?

Cor blimey says Spudgy don't you know the kings English? trouble and strife his wife.

Aah I see now Mon Spudgy, I think we should send a message to Monsieur Dr Brown

What message is that then? asks Spudgy

Never mind Mon Spudgy can you please request Monsieur Dr Brown to call to see me at his convenience.

Off Spudgy flew to the forest but not before popping in to pay his regards to the new Linnet family.

Hi Lenny brought you some caterpillars for the new bin lids, but can't stop gotta get a message to old Brownie.

Thanks for popping by and for the gifts much appreciated Spudgy says Leonard

Spudgy arrived at the oak tree as Dr Brown is sat outside his door reading a book.

Afternoon Brownie, ave a message from old red, he said you need to call to see him at your convenience.

Not wishing to engage in any conversation with Spudgy, Dr Brown simply replied, do tell the Marquis Morningcall that I shall honour his request and pay a visit

Im confused says Spudgy but I will tell old red wot you said.

Marquis Morningcall was sat in his usual place with one eye open when Spudgy appeared, that was quick Mon Spudgy.

I gave old Brownie the message and he said he was going the carzey

I don't understand Mon Spudgy what is this carzey?

You know says Spudgy la toilette he said to tell you he will pay a visit

I think Mon Spudgy that your interpretation of paying a visit is different than that of Monsieur Dr Brown.

Later in the day Dr Brown arrived at the farmhouse, a visit that was noticed by Matt the barn owl.

Good afternoon Marquis Morningcall says Dr Brown

And a very good afternoon to you too Monsieur Dr Brown and thank you for paying me the visit.

What's owl this then says Matt as he settles down on the fence.

Aah Matt Im glad that you have appeared as the Marquis Morningcall had invited me here for what I trust is important news?

Wee the news is that Mon Spudgy overheard the town people saying they are taking over thee farm and will be re-wilding the fields.

Re-wilding? asks Matt

Im not entirely sure what that is says Dr Brown but I will have a look in my 'big book of all things' and let you owl know, drat I mean let you all know.

Matt, says Dr Brown we really need to sit down one day and discuss the usage of the noun owl.

Anytime your free Dr Brown owl be available says Matt

Dr Brown thought to say something back but decided against it and bid his farewell then flew back to the majestic oak to consult his 'big book of all things' he settled down to consult the book but is disturbed by a commotion outside, what on earth is all this hullabaloo says Dr Brown

Beg to disturb you Dr Brown says Smalls the little owl, it's Jasper the jackdaw he keeps popping into my home and stealing things. He took Miriam's feather duvet and I just caught him stealing the mop bucket.

Jasper is this true what Smalls is saying asked Dr Brown?

Well kind of guvnor, I like to borrow things bit like Bertie the badger can't help me self just a habit I have.

Jasper if you are borrowing things you must obtain permission to do so and you must return them within a reasonable time. Now I suggest that you return the duvet and the mop bucket at once, the duvet I understand but why take a mop bucket?

I err liked the colour guvnor but I will take em back

Smalls, says Dr Brown I have a new mortice lock that you can have and that will stop any future borrowing should Jasper go wandering again. Now Im returning to my 'big book of all things' I have urgent business to contend too.

Dr Brown returned to his 'big book of all things' re, re, regeneration, rehousing, re wilding aah here it is. Well, thought Dr Brown this is excellent, excellent indeed I shall summon a meeting to relay what I have learnt.

Later that day with everyone assembled in the clearance around the majestic oak Dr Brown gave the news.

We have heard that new towns people are taking over the farm says Dr Brown and are to bring a new approach to managing the farm and surrounding fields. It is my understanding having consulted my 'big book of all things' that new ponds might be dug in the fields and more meadows created and the hedgerows that we have so few of could be coming back.

Great shouts Leonard the linnet my little uns will be able to build their homes here instead of moving away.

We may also say Dr Brown see new members arrive in our community such as pigs.

Bang goes the neighbourhood says Sylvester

Of course, says Dr Brown we will have wait to see what happens but for now that is what I have been told.

Things remained quiet over the next few months till one morning Hamilton came charging through the forest shouting they are back, they are right behind me Im done for.

Dr Brown was snoozing in his bed and threw on his dressing gown and came to the door still wearing his nightcap 'what is all this shouting, what on earth is going on.

Hamilton's shouting had alerted everyone in the forest. They are here he shouts I have to hide before they see me again.

What makes you think they are after you Hamilton? asks Dr Brown

The pigs lost his head shouts Bertie

I shall fetch an apple said Sylvester adding Salade Lyonnaise a fine starter with a glass of Beaujolais.

Im out of here shouts Hamilton its everyone for themselves as he makes for the East of the forest

A few minutes later Ecclefechan enters the clearance and tells Dr Brown that the town people are erecting signs that have the fruit of his oak tree home on them.

Are you sure asks Dr Brown, you mean they have picture of acorns on them?

Well they look like them and those them leaves but can't say for definite I know my great cousin Hamish of the clan Hamish has them around where he lives.

This I have to see says Sylvester, clan Hamish indeed

A party of volunteers were sent to the outskirts of the forest to see what the signs are.

It looks very much like Ecclefechan was correct says Reginald they are very much like the majestic oak.

The news is relayed to Dr Brown who asks everyone to remain while he consults his 'big book of all things' again. After about ten minutes Dr Brown emerges to tell the assembled that the signs belong to an organisation called the National trust and that they must be looking after the forest and meadows which means the forest might not be pulled down and the towns people might not be building houses on all of the fields.

Before I confirm the news, I must see the Marquis Morningcall as he has ears to the ground, I shall go there right away.

Dr Brown arrived at the farm as Marquis Morningcall and Spudgy were discussing matters involving the farm.

Im telling yer red me ole mate he was on the old dog and bone having a good old rabbit and pork about that leaking roof an getting it fixed.

Good afternoon Marquis Morningcall Im sorry to interrupt says Dr Brown.

Not at tall Monsieur Dr Brown Mon Spudge was just telling me

Err Spudgy

My apologies again Mon Spudgy, yes as I was saying Mon Spudgy was telling me of thee new owner having the hay barn roof repaired

Well that is good news says Dr Brown it means that the farm is going to be looked after.

Means a warmer Mickey mouse for me and me china plates says Spudgy anyway Brownie wot brings you over here?

I have come to enquire if the Marquis Morningcall has heard anymore of the re-wilding of the fields.

I thought you would have heard news from your adjointe Matt? Says the Marquis Morningcall

No chance of that, it's all treacle and turtle dove said Spudgy

What? asks Dr Brown puzzled

I think what Mon Spudgy is trying to say is that Matt has a new sweetheart and it is amour says Marquis Morningcall

Matts in love said Spudgy

Well as good as this double act is I must know if the forest is no longer at risk.

Indeed, it is not said Marquis Morningcall, my understanding of these matters is that there is fleurs rarers, le triton and thee rouge ecureuil.

He means April showers, newts and Harlow and his china plates says Spudgy

It is May says Dr Brown so what has April showers got to do with it?

Mon Spudgy means thee flowers says Marquis Morningcall

Dr Brown still puzzled by the conversation leaves for the forest and asks for everyone to be assemble at six o'clock for the news.

Well said Dr Brown we are not having to leave this our home

Does this mean they are not coming to get me asks Hamilton?

I have just heard said Sylvester that the towns people are renaming the Plough Inn the Boars Head

Stop it Sylvester, said Dr Brown, no Hamilton they were never coming to get you, not then not now not ever

What a shame says Sylvester, we should still hold a barbecue to celebrate I shall fetch the teriyaki sauce it is delicious with pork ribs.

Ignore him Hamilton says Reginald

Yes, said Dr Brown we will all need to get on together we have been given this great opportunity

In the magnificent words of my ancestor Rupert hare of Dumbarton said Ecclefechan

Not now came the unanimous response of all gathered.

New beginnings

More ponds were dug in the meadows and new hedgerows planted with native species providing safe refuge helping the wild life to move from one habitat to another. The hedgerows also aided pollination of the crops and acted as barriers for the livestock that had been introduced as part of the re-wilding of the fields.

What became of the original occupants of the forest and farms

Old Dr Brown informed the inhabitants that he was to retire to his cousins' home in Hampshire and announced. It is with a heaviness of heart that I leave the majestic oak and the forest that has been my home for as long as I can rightly recall, but I leave you in the capable talons of my nephew young Dr Brown whom I have bequeathed my 'big book of all things'. I have every confidence in his ability to act in the best interest of you the forest community

Where is he coming from? asked Smalls the little owl

He was, said Dr Brown working in the owl hospital drat I mean the old hospital but it is being pulled down and so he is to join you all later this morning.

Matt the barn owl moved several miles away with his partner Martha where they set up home on an old farm and reared a family. Each bedtime he tells them stories of the good owl days.

Ecclefechan was afforded a position in the forest nursery where he tells the young uns dashing tales of his ancestors including Rupert hare of Dumbarton till they all fall asleep.

Remarkable said Maple rabbit how they all go asleep for him

They ave no choice said Bertie the badger, adding I can barely keep me eye lids open when he tells them their stories.

Bertie remained at the forest for a short while but decided to seek pastures new and set off for Gloucester where he said there are fewer blooming cows, before leaving he left Bruce the hedgehog a bag of worms with a note saying Brucie bonus.

Harlow and Paramour and the rest of the reds flourished as the greys were banished from the forest. The greys made their way to distant towns to establish their own communities.

Ruby and Bertram no longer watch over the young branches, that task now allocated to others but they are often asked to give talks about the old days.

Jack by the hedge continues to scurry in and out of the now extensive hedgerows.

Jasper the jackdaw left the forest after Chaz the crow stole his door mat.

Sylvester and Hamilton settled their differences and opened a successful truffle company called Sylvester's. Hamilton works an average forty hours per week searching for truffles whilst Sylvester relaxes in the meadow citing that as he is a silent partner he is staying silent and out of the way.

Besides, said Sylvester someone has to cook the books, I mean do the books

But, asked Reginald rabbit 'the company is called Sylvester's so how can you be a silent partner?

My dear fellow, said Sylvester the company name is irrelevant and what I do is purely for health and wellbeing reasons. What health and wellbeing asked Reginald?

The pig's health and wellbeing of course responded Sylvester Im trying to keep him in shape through daily exercise, dear me one would think that Im trying to exploit the poor fellow.

Reginald, Maple and their family continue to live at the warren the kits still attend the local school.

Willie the weasel left for Australia and stowed on board a ferry but ended up on the Isle of Wight.

How do you know he ended up on the Isle of White? asked Jill the stoat

Well, said Maurice the moorhen, Chas the crow told me and Arthur he was visiting his cousin who has a home on the roof of Parkhurst prison and said he was mooching around one morning looking for grubs when he heard a whistle and it was Willie

G'day Chaz how ya going cobber?

What are you doing here asked Chaz, I thought you were going home to Australia.

Well said Willie, really confusing to say the least I must be a right drongo, knew it wasn't Oz and reckoned I must be in Tasmania but not seen any roos about. Guess I will stick around here till I find my feet then set off for Oz.

So where are you staying? asked Chaz

Im camped by a billabong it will do for now, pass on my regards to the other poms when you get back said Willie.

Marquis Morningcall was retired from the farm and replaced by a younger rooster

Morning red you took over from old red then asked Spudgy?

If you mean the Marquis Morningcall, wee I have taken up thee position.

Well then red me ole mate we are going have plenty of time to rabbit and pork

What is this red and thee rabbit and pork, kindly address me by my title duke de Richelieu Versailles.

Cor bit of a mouthful that red, said Spudgy adding isn't Versailles that place where the townie with one eye walked around with his hand inside his vest?

I think you anglaise sparrow thee townie with one eye as you call him is your own Lord Nelson not the glorious Emperor Napoléon Bonaparte in his splendid palace garden.

Nah said Spudgy, Nelson was on a ship not in some garden ow ever nice it was.

Spudgy knew it was not going to be the same without the Marquis Morningcall and decided to leave.

Hi Lennie said Spudgy to Leonard the linnet, Im getting off, ole place aint the same without ole red

You heading back to the east end then Spudgy?

No Lennie going to me ole china plates hotel on the coast, fancy some sea air for a change

Watch them seagulls Spudgy I heard they are worse thieves than that Jackdaw Jasper, though heard he has taken himself off he didn't like a taste of his own medicine.

They will ave to be up early to get one over on me Lennie, said Spudgy you take care me ole china.

You to Spudgy said Leonard with a tear in his eye

And so Spudgy set off for Clacton-on-Sea whistling maybe it's because Im a Londoner as he flew over the meadow for the last time to begin the next chapter in his life

The End

www.ingramcontent.com/pod-product-compliance
Ingram Content Group UK Ltd.
Pitfield, Milton Keynes, MK11 3LW, UK
UKHW020954280325
456847UK00006B/739